Published in Canada and the USA in 2021 by Groundwood Books
English translation copyright © 2021 by Andrée Poulin

First published in French as *Enterrer la lune* copyright © 2019 by la courte échelle,
an imprint of Groupe d'édition la courte échelle

Groundwood Books / House of Anansi Press
groundwoodbooks.com

Groundwood Books respectfully acknowledges that the land on which we operate is the Traditional
Territory of many Nations, including the Anishinabeg, the Wendat and the Haudenosaunee. It is also
the Treaty Lands of the Mississaugas of the Credit.

We gratefully acknowledge for their financial support of our publishing program the Canada Council
for the Arts, the Ontario Arts Council and the Government of Canada.

Canada Council **Conseil des Arts**
for the Arts **du Canada**

ONTARIO ARTS COUNCIL
CONSEIL DES ARTS DE L'ONTARIO

an Ontario government agency
un organisme du gouvernement de l'Ontario

With the participation of the Government of Canada
Avec la participation du gouvernement du Canada

Canadä

Library and Archives Canada Cataloguing in Publication
Title: Burying the moon / Andrée Poulin ; illustrations by Sonali Zohra.
Other titles: Enterrer la lune. English
Names: Poulin, Andrée, author. | Zohra, Sonali, illustrator.
Description: Translation of: Enterrer la lune.
Identifiers: Canadiana (print) 20200390724 | Canadiana (ebook) 20200390775 | ISBN
9781773066042 (hardcover) | ISBN 9781773066035 (EPUB)
Classification: LCC PS8581.O837 E5813 2021 | DDC jC843/.54—dc23

The illustrations were created digitally.
Design by Julie Massy
Printed and bound in Canada

Groundwood Books is a Global Certified Accessible™ (GCA by Benetech) publisher. An ebook version
of this book that meets stringent accessibility standards is available to students and readers with print
disabilities.

Groundwood Books is committed to protecting our natural environment. This book is made of material
from well-managed FSC®-certified forests, recycled materials, and other controlled sources.

MIX
Paper from
responsible sources
FSC® C016245

Written by Andrée Poulin

Burying the Moon

Illustrated by Sonali Zohra

Groundwood Books
House of Anansi Press
Toronto / Berkeley

For Angèle, whom I admire greatly for her passionate commitment to improving the lives of women in India.
—AP

*"Three things cannot be long hidden:
the sun, the moon, and the truth."*
Buddha

In the Field of Shame

High
in the shimmering sky
   the silver
      moon
      gazes
         at a
      gloomy
      girl.

Head back
forehead furrowed
Latika sticks her
tongue out
at the moon.

Each night
Latika wishes
for the dark.
A deep
   deep
   dark.
A night
without light.
A night
without moon.

Every night
Latika follows
   her sister
   her mother
   her neighbors.

She follows
   the silent women
   treading the path
   to the field
   where nothing grows.

Every night
  women and girls
  trudge to
  the field
  of Shame.
Always at night.
  Never during the day.

On the outskirts
  of the village
in the deserted field
  shadows
  squat on the ground.

Heads down
  saris lifted
worried women
watch
for danger.

The women and the girls
don't look at each other
don't look at the moon.
Crouching in silence
they do
  what
they need
        to do.

Burying the Moon

Latika's mother
says nervously:
"Hurry, hurry!"

Ranjini, Latika's sister,
says impatiently:
"We're always waiting for you!"

Latika sighs
and whispers fiercely:
"I'm trying.
I want to.
But my belly won't listen."

Latika hates
having to whisper
when she wants
to scream.

Scream
   rude
   crude
   words
   at the moon.
Scream
   insults.

Because this cruel moon
    shines too much light
on the crouching women.

Because this brazen moon
        won't let her
            hide.

Every night
in the field
   of Shame
Latika has only
   one thought
   one wish:
   to bury the moon.

Drowning Jealousy

Every morning
Latika goes to the river
  with her bucket empty.
Every morning
Latika returns from the river
  with her bucket full.

On the way home
        she walks
            slowly.
Neck stiff.
Back straight.
A spilled bucket
means
    starting
        over.

Every morning
Latika has
   to hurry
   to the river.
Despite her rush
   to get there
   she takes
   the long way.

The long way
lets her avoid
the silly
carefree
boys.

These
happy-go-lucky
barefoot boys
   are always
      having
         fun.

Boys without a care
who never
carry
empty buckets
   or
   full buckets.

Lucky boys
who never
    have to hide.
Who never
    have to go
    to the field
    of Shame.

Every morning
on the way
    to the river
        jealousy
stings Latika.

Jealousy
    as cruel
    as a bee's sting.

Latika dips her bucket
    into the roiling
                river.

She wishes
she could drown
    her jealousy.

Fragile but Strong

Latika hurries.
She doesn't want
to keep her ammamma
                    waiting.

Latika's grandma
rarely leaves her bed.
Today
again
Ammamma has a high fever.

Too weak
    to rise,
Ammamma is never
too weak
    to smile.
Even when she is
        in a bad way
Ammamma never forgets
                to say
            thank you.

Latika thinks
her ammamma
is frail but brave
fragile but strong.

Sorrowful and Inconsolable

After Ammamma's smile
   Latika must face
   Aunty Nita's tears.

Latika brings water
to her sorrowful
     and inconsolable
     aunty.

Aunty Nita cries constantly.
From morning to evening.
From evening to morning.

As soon as she sees Latika
Aunty Nita says
   for the thousandth time:
   "I want my son.
   I want my Jamal."

For many
    many
    months
Aunty Nita has repeated
the same sad sentences
       has wished
the same useless wish:
     "I want my son.
     I want my Jamal."

Latika pours water
    from the river
into Aunty Nita's jug.

Latika whispers
    gentle words
comforting words.
But Aunty Nita
    won't listen.
    Can't hear.
Inconsolable people
have no ears.

Pure Joy

Every morning
Latika runs to school.
She is always excited
    to go to class.

In school
    Latika forgets Ammamma's illness
        forgets Aunty Nita's tears
        forgets the moon
        forgets Shame.

Confident
  and
  cheerful
Latika reels off
the capital cities:
Beijing
Beirut
Bogotá
Bujumbura

In a fearless voice
  Latika reels off
  the times tables:
  9 × 6 = 54
  10 × 6 = 60
  11 × 6 = 66

With a focused expression
and a steady hand
Latika writes in her notebook
the awesome story
        of Gandhi
    who walked almost
  400 kilometers
            to collect salt
        from the sea.

In school
Latika smiles
        often —
        almost
        always!

In school
Latika loves to
        learn
        think
        understand.

In school
Latika
is able to
find
pure joy.

Everything Changed

Latika's big sister
also loves to
    learn
    think
    understand.

Ranjini
is often at the top
    of her class.

But now
Latika has to use the
      past tense.
Ranjini loved to learn.
Ranjini used to be at the top
of her class.
Not anymore.
Everything has changed.

A few weeks ago
  Ranjini had to stop
      learning
     had to stop
    going to school.

The day Latika's sister
      turned twelve
everything changed.
Everything.

When Anger Sticks to the Heart

Before
when they wove baskets
Latika
and Ranjini
     sang songs
       told jokes
teased each other.

With all this
  giggling
  and
  teasing
the two sisters
  would forget
they were working.

All this banter
    and
    laughter
made their baskets
  even prettier.

That was before.
Now
everything has changed.

In Padaram
   girls
who are almost
   women
   stop going
   to school.

When Ranjini turned twelve
   she protested
      pleaded
      ranted.

She also
   sobbed.
   But it was no use.

Her father said:
   "No.
   No.
   No.
You are a woman
      now.
   It's not appropriate
   at your age!"

Since she stopped school
Ranjini
　　does not talk
　　does not sing
　　does not laugh.

Since she stopped school
Ranjini
weaves her baskets
　　　　in silence.

Since she stopped school
Ranjini
　　kicks.

Kicks the hens
　　on the road
kicks the goats
　　on the road
kicks the dust
　　on the road
　　as if the dust
has insulted her.

Since she stopped school
anger sticks
to Ranjini's heart.

"Appropriate…"
Appropriate?
Latika doesn't
understand
the word.
But she
understands
why school
is forbidden
for girls
who turn
twelve.

It's because
of
Shame.

Often and Never

In school, Latika
is often
thirsty.
Often.

Dry mouth.
Dry lips.
Often.

In school, Latika never drinks water.
   Never.
   Not
   one
   single
   drop.
Not even
   when the sun boils hot.
Never.

If Latika drank water
   she would need to pee.

But in Latika's school
   in Padaram
   there are no toilets
      and no girls
         older than
            twelve.

Stop Time...

Latika knows that
when a girl
turns twelve
she becomes
a young woman.

Latika has noticed
the changes
in Ranjini's body.

Latika knows that
at twelve years old
a girl can be a mother.

In her class
where Latika finds
pure joy
where she learns
and learns to think
and learns to understand...
Latika wishes
    to stop time
    so that she will
                never
                never
                    turn twelve.

Latika wants to stay a little girl
            to stay in school.

With His Lips and His Eyes

This morning
Latika has no time
   to walk to the river
      to fetch water.

The head of the village of Padaram
has called the villagers
to gather round
the big banyan tree.

When the sarpanch speaks
    the villagers obey.

Under the shade
of the big banyan tree
   stands a stranger
      from the city.

The villagers whisper
   and hover.

The crowd wavers
    between apprehension
   and anticipation.

Will the news be
   good or bad
  for Padaram?

As solemn as a judge
the sarpanch
   swells his chest
   and states:
"It is my great pleasure
   to welcome
   to Padaram
   Mister Samir
   a very-important-government-official."

Latika watches the stranger
her mouth open
   in fascination.

In the village
   no one wears
   a polka-dot bow tie.

In the village
   no one
   smiles like
   this Mister Samir
   with his lips
      AND
   with his eyes!

Mister Samir greets the crowd:
"The government wants to help your village.
I am here to listen.
What do you wish
   for Padaram?"

Latika wants to cheer
and clap
for this surprising
Mister Samir
for his friendly voice
and
smiling eyes.

Latika wants to cheer
and clap
for this surprising
Mister Samir
who is here…
to listen!

Not like the sarpanch
   who always says:
   "Listen to me!
   Listen to me!"

The men ask for electricity for Padaram.
The women ask for a well for Padaram.
The boys ask for cricket balls.
The girls ask for nothing.

Latika is on
pins and needles.
She whispers
in her mother's ear.

Her mother
shakes her head:
 "NO!
  NO!
  NO!
We don't talk about that.
Especially not to a
 a very-important-government-official.
Especially not
to someone
 so elegant
 who wears
 a polka-dot bow tie!"

Latika clenches her fists
  muzzles her anger.

It's so hard
to stay silent
when you have
important things
          to say.
Important things
 that everyone
  stays silent
         about.

Catching the Moon on a Stick

Every evening after dinner
Latika and Ranjini weave baskets.

Latika tickles her sister.
        "Stop!" says Ranjini.

Since her sister
refuses to laugh
Latika decides to
                speak
            seriously.

"Ranjini, I have an idea..."
Her big sister doesn't answer.
Latika goes on.
        "What if we showed
        the field of Shame
        to the very-important-official-
        from-the-government?
        What if we explained?
        What if we asked..."

Ranjini stops weaving
    and lets out an exasperated sigh.
        "He'll never listen.
        And even if he listened
        he wouldn't understand.
        You would have more chance
                of catching the moon on a stick."

Jealousy Stings Again

For Latika
each visit
to Nuppapuram
    is definitely pleasant
and definitely unpleasant.

The walk to Nuppapuram
is definitely pleasant.
With lots of time
for
babbling
jabbering
and
chit-chattering.

Sometimes —
        not often —
Latika's mother
        will sing!

The Nuppapuram market
is definitely pleasant.
Vibrant colors
tempting smells
women hollering
        whistling
    and laughing.

The Nuppapuram market
is also unpleasant.
So many customers
who don't want to pay
            a fair price
for the straw baskets
that Latika and her sister
                have spent hours
                    weaving.

But for Latika
the hardest part
the most
unpleasant part
of her visits
to Nuppapuram
is the jealousy.

Jealousy
    as cruel
    as a bee
stings her
each time
she walks past
the Nuppapuram school.

In the Nuppapuram classrooms
there are girls
who are older
    than twelve.

To Be a Goat

There are days
when Latika
wants
to be a goat.

It's silly.
She knows.

But a goat
isn't disturbed
        by the
        moon.

Stupid Question

Three days later
Mister Samir comes back
   to Padaram
   with another stranger
   from the city.

As solemn as a judge
the sarpanch announces:
"This man is an engineer."

Without thinking
without hesitating
Latika dares to ask:
"What is an engineer?"

The sarpanch's answer hurts
like a slap to the face:
"Don't ask stupid questions!"

Latika clenches her fists
      muzzles her anger.

She hesitates.
Should she be mad at the sarpanch
for saying her question was stupid?
Or should she be mad at her teacher
   for claiming
   that there is no such thing
   as a stupid question?

Just a Piece of Gum…

Mister Samir
      and
the engineer
roam the village
looking for the best spot
to drill a well.

A flock of little kids —
      mostly boys —
follows the city men.

Latika is not a little kid.
Latika is not a boy.
Yet she dares
    to follow
      the two men
        from a distance.

As pushy
        and
    bossy
as a commander
in the army
the sarpanch
    tries to chase away
        the curious children.

Mister Samir laughs and shouts:
"Leave them be!
I like children,
    especially
curious children!"

When Mister Samir is done exploring
      he takes off his polka-dot bow tie
            and gets a ball from the truck
            to play cricket with the boys.

The sarpanch
   is speechless
with surprise.

He can't believe
      a very-important-government-official
      would jostle and scramble
      and scuffle and tumble
               with a gaggle
                     of dirty kids.

Disheveled
      and rumpled
      and dusty
Mister Samir
the very-important-government-official
giggles like a little boy
when he misses the ball.
From under the shade of the big banyan tree
Latika watches
the boys
laugh and play.
She wishes
she could play.
But she doesn't
         dare.

When the game is over
Mister Samir gives out sticks
      of gum.

The boys whoop
      and jump.
   Yay! Yippee!

Latika grumbles:
"It's not a diamond
                  necklace.
It's just a
   tiny
   useless
   stick of gum."

Jealousy
stings Latika again.
Jealousy
   can be persistent
   as a bee.

An Engineer Is...

But...
suddenly
unexpectedly
amazingly
Mister Samir walks
   to the big banyan tree
      to talk
      to Latika!

She can't believe her eyes.

Mister Samir
   hands her
a stick of gum.

Latika is flabbergasted,
feet
frozen
to the spot.

Mister Samir
is so close
she can see
very clearly
how he smiles
   with his lips
      AND
   with his eyes!

Mister Samir says:
"An engineer is someone who builds
                    something useful."

Latika snaps out
        of her daze.
She takes the gum
from Mister Samir.
She whispers,
        "Thank you."
But Latika's
        thank-you
                is not
        for the gum.

Waiting and Watching

The next day
Mister Samir comes back
   to Padaram
   in a red truck
     as massive as a small hill.

From this
red truck
the village men
unload:
   one drill rig
   dozens of bags of concrete
   dozens of long silver pipes.

All of this
   will be used
   to dig a
   well
   for Padaram.

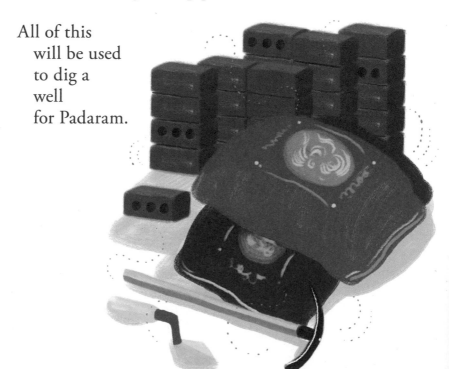

Latika hovers around
the construction site
where the men are working.
She waits for the best time
to approach Mister Samir
to tell him
the important things
that everyone else
        stays silent
            about.

Latika watches.
And waits.
Waits.
And watches.

On the construction site
Mister Samir is as active
            as an ant.

Conscientious and tireless
Mister Samir
guides and encourages the workers.

Latika herself
    grows
    antsy.

When can she
    finally speak
to Mister Samir?

At lunch break
under the shade
of the big banyan tree
the workers relax
       and relish
       their rice
       and curry.

Latika sneaks to the
   gigantic red truck
   and quietly opens
              the door.

Helping herself up
with her hands
       and
       her feet
          she climbs the steps
              to reach
                 the passenger's seat.

At the end of the day
when Mister Samir
gets in the truck
Latika will be there
       and will finally
       speak to him.

Searching for Strong Words

Through the
long
hot
interminable afternoon
Latika hides
in the gigantic red truck.

She watches.
And waits.

She tries not to think
   that she is hot.
       Tries not to think
   that she is thirsty.

So she forces herself
to think of the best words to say.
She searches for strong and
heart-touching
words to say to Mister Samir.

Words to express these important things
that everyone
   stays silent
       about.
After many long hot hours
the door of the gigantic red truck
opens.

Latika sees
a white shirt
   but
she doesn't see
Mister Samir's smile.

She sees
   the startled
      stare
of the city engineer.
And behind him
she sees
the livid look
of the sarpanch.

Like an angry rooster
the sarpanch
      crows
       and
      squawks
       and
      flaps
   his arms.

Latika panics.
She tumbles
out of the
   gigantic red truck and
      flees
      the furious shouts
of the frenzied sarpanch.

Silence Hurts

Latika hides behind
her sleeping
ammamma's bed.

She rolls up
   into a ball.
     A small
       ball.

Eyes closed
fists clenched
Latika trembles
for a long
    long
     time.

No.
There were no
  blows
    and
    kicks
    and
  stones
    and
  sticks.

But
yes.
Latika feels pain.

Pain
because she could not tell
Mister Samir
the important things
that everyone
    stays silent
            about.

For Latika
    this forced silence is worse
        than
    blows
        and
        kicks
        and
    stones
        and
    sticks.

Under the Haystack...

The women have returned
from the field
    of Shame.
  The men snore.
The chicks snooze.
The dogs slumber.
The whole village
    of Padaram
        sleeps.

But Latika can't sleep.
Thoughts swirl in her head:
   the well...
     Ranjini's anger...
       her own anger...
         in the field
           of Shame.

Latika silently
rises from her bed.
She runs through the village
to the site where the well lies
   half-drilled.

Tonight
   the moon is not round
   like an orange.
   The moon has the gentle curve
   of a banana.

But…
the moonbeams are still
   so very silver
   so very bright
and they perfectly
         light up
         the site.

Head back
forehead furrowed
Latika sticks her
tongue out
   at the moon
   at its cruel
         gleam.

Latika watches
and waits.
Waits
and watches.

Suddenly…
Finally!
A flock
of fluffy cumulus clouds
   conceals
   the moon.

Finally!
Welcome
   sweet darkness.

Latika leaps
   and grabs a pick
   and runs.

She hides the pick
   under a haystack.

Then she runs back
   to the construction site.

She takes two wooden planks
   and flees again.

Under another pile of hay
       farther away
  she hides her planks.

Weary
but happy
Latika goes
   back to bed.

For the first time
   in a long time
she falls asleep
       smiling.

A Bundle of Fears

The following night
    Latika goes out
           again.
Again
she waits
   till the men snore
   till the chicks snooze
   till the dogs slumber
   till the whole village
        of Padaram
      is sleeping.

Pick in hand
Latika walks
very quietly
to the field
of Shame.

High
in the shimmering sky
  the silver
    moon
      gazes
       at a
      fearful
      girl.

Latika trembles.
Is it from the cold?
   Is it from fear?
      Is it both?

Yes…
Latika is afraid.
Afraid of snakes.
Afraid of scorpions.
Afraid of humans.
Afraid of those
   who would try
     to stop her.
But no…
   Latika won't
   be stopped!

Fear Fades

The first
strikes of the pick
    are the hardest.
Little by little, Latika warms up.
Little by little, Latika stops trembling.
Little by little, the hole grows bigger.
Little by little, her fear gets smaller.

In the field
        of Shame
Latika murmurs to herself.
She whispers
Mister Samir's words:
    "An engineer is someone who builds
                            something useful."

Head back
forehead furrowed
Latika calls out
    to the
    cheeky
    moon:
    "I am an engineer!"

Happy Dance

The well is dug
the pump is pumping!

Today in Padaram
water flows!
Today in Padaram
joy swirls!
Today in Padaram
villagers twirl!

The men clap.
The women sing.
The children dance.

Grinning widely
polka-dot bow tie
askew
Mister Samir dances
with the children.

Thrilled
  with this
  new well
Latika claps
  her hands.

No more long treks to the river.
No more heavy bucket.
No more sore neck.

Latika hops
  and skips
  with the happy-go-lucky boys.
Latika laughs
  and dances
  with the carefree kids.

The Party Is Over

Suddenly…
   the sarpanch
   stops the music.
With his cantankerous voice
with his bad-news tone
   he declares:
      "The party is over."

In his hand
the sarpanch
holds…
   a pick.

Latika wants to run.

But
  her
    feet
      are
        frozen.

Her heart beats
so loudly
she can't
  hear
  her
  thoughts.

The sarpanch
throws the pick
    at the feet
of Latika's mother.

"I found this behind your house. Thief!"

Latika's mother
covers her face
with her hands.
Then
  she
    bursts
      into
        tears.

What Will the Punishment Be?

Latika stands
    in front of her mother.
Faces the crowd.
Faces the sarpanch.

    Her arms tremble.
    Her legs tremble.
Her whole body trembles.

In a quavering voice
  Latika says:
"My mother has done nothing
    wrong.
  I have done nothing
    wrong.
  I did not steal this pick
  I simply borrowed it."

Latika takes
a deep breath
and says:
"I borrowed this pick
to work like an engineer.
To build something useful."

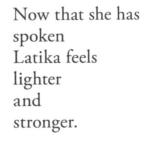

Now that she has
spoken
Latika feels
lighter
and
stronger.

Now...
Latika waits.

She knows
she will be punished.
What will her punishment be?
She doesn't know.

Ruined Forever

The sarpanch
   bellows
      like a
         bull.
His words tangle
      and tumble
in a vicious
      stream.
THIEF
   LIAR
      SHAMELESS
         DISRESPECTFUL
            UNFORGIVABLE

Firmly
   but
politely
Mister Samir interrupts
         the sarpanch.
   "Please.
   Please.
   Allow me…"

Mister Samir
the very-important-government-official
motions to Latika:
   "Follow me."

Latika walks
    past the silent crowd
    past the disapproval
    past the angry faces.

Latika feels
terribly guilty.
    It's her fault
    the party
has ended
    so soon
        and
    in blame
        and
    shame.

Latika also feels
    sick at heart
    that because of a
badly hidden pick
    her beautiful
        project
            is ruined
                forever.

Bow Tie on a Branch

Under the big banyan tree
  far from the crowd
  far from the sarpanch
Mister Samir asks Latika:
"Why did you take that pick?"

Mister Samir doesn't smile.
  Not with his lips.
  Not with his eyes.
  But his voice
    is
  gentle.

Head hung low
Latika stays
    silent.

Mister Samir asks again:
"Why did you take that pick?"

Latika murmurs:
  "My mother says it's not polite
  to speak about Shame
  to a very-important-government-official
  who comes from far away
    and
  who is so elegant
  with his bow tie."

Calmly
Mister Samir
  takes off
    his polka-dot
      bow tie
      and throws it
        very high.

      So high
      that the polka-dot
      bow tie
      gets caught
      in a branch
      of the big banyan tree.

Astonished
by this boldness
    Latika
    stares.

Mister Samir tells her:
"Forget who I am."

Then he says words
that Latika finds
    so simple
            yet
    so beautiful.

He says:
    "I'm listening. Don't be afraid."

Latika opens her mouth
but the words
            won't
    come out.

Latika pinches her arm
forces her mouth
    to say
these important things
that everyone
        stays silent
                about.

For Ranjini

I borrowed the pick
for my sister Ranjini
who kicks the hens
   on the road
who kicks the goats
   on the road
who kicks the dust
   on the road
   as if the dust
has insulted her.

My big sister
loves to learn.
But her learning days
            are over.
She can't go to school
            anymore.

I borrowed the pick
for my sister Ranjini
who doesn't hide
   her anger
during the day
      but
hides her tears
   at night.

All this
because
at our school
there is nowhere
to do…
　　you know what.

I borrowed the pick
because it's not
　　fair
that there are toilets
　　in Nuppapuram
　　　but not
　　in Padaram.

Hesitant and Wavering (1)

Mister Samir
doesn't look at Latika.
He fiddles
with a pebble.

Latika
hesitates
    and
wavers.
"Shall I go on?"

Mister Samir nods.
"Yes. I'm listening."

For Ammamma

I borrowed the pick
for my ammamma
who was bitten
by a scorpion
in the field
    of Shame.

Since then
my ammamma
has had
a fever.
Since then
my ammamma
    is too sick
    to leave
    her bed.

All this
because
in Padaram
there is nowhere
to do...
    you know what.

Hesitant and Wavering (2)

Mister Samir says
     nothing.
Sitting cross-legged
he stares at
  the ground
    as if he's looking
      for answers
     in the
       dirt.

Latika
hesitates
  and
wavers.
"Shall I go on?"

Mister Samir nods.
"Yes. I'm listening."

For Aunty Nita

I borrowed the pick
for Aunty Nita
who cries all the time.
From morning to evening.
From evening to morning.
Since she lost
   her little Jamal.

When Jamal started to walk
Aunty Nita laughed
to see her son
    chase the chicks
  with wobbly
  baby steps.

Jamal had just
  started talking
  when the fever
    got him.

The doctor came.
But he didn't really help us
  with his complicated
  words:
    Filth.
    Hygiene.
    Sanitation.
    Infection.
    Parasites.

Complicated words
  as punishing
  as crushing
  as blame.
Aunty Nita sold three goats
  to pay for the medication.
But it was
       too
         late.

Never again
did little Jamal
  chase
  chicks
with wobbly
baby steps.

Jamal, so perky
    so bouncy
    stopped smiling
    stopped eating
    stopped breathing.

All this
because
in Padaram
there is nowhere
to do…
    you know what.

Hesitant and Wavering (3)

Mister Samir still
won't
look
at Latika.

She doesn't know what he thinks.
She doesn't know what to think.

Did she choose the right words?
   Strong
      and
heart-touching
   words to explain…
            prove…
            convince?
Latika
hesitates
   and
wavers.
"Shall I go on?"

Mister Samir nods.
"Yes. I'm listening."

Burying the Moon

"I borrowed the pick
  to bury the moon.

"Don't tell me.
I know
it's impossible
to bury the moon.

"But if it was possible
I would do it.
Yes, I would really do it."

Mister Samir lifts his head and asks:
"Why?
  Why...
  do you want to bury the moon?"

Latika hesitates.
Even though Mister Samir
is listening carefully
he is not smiling
with his lips
    nor
with his eyes.

Latika is afraid
    afraid to dare
    afraid to fail
    afraid to hope.

She lifts her head
   and sees
      the polka-dot bow tie
         hanging from the branch
            of the big banyan tree.

That tiny
   polka-dot bow tie
      blowing in the
      breeze
      gives her courage.

Latika tells the
very-important-government-official:
"Mister Samir
please come with me.
I will show you why
         I want to
   bury the moon."

Under the Hay

Latika and Mister Samir
walk in silence.

Suddenly
Latika veers off
the path
and stops
in front
of a pile of hay.

In a low voice
she confesses:
"I borrowed a pick…
and I also borrowed these planks.
But the sarpanch
   doesn't know."

Mister Samir
says nothing.
But Latika sees
a quick smile
   quickly hidden.

Where Men Never Go...

Latika takes Mister Samir
where men
never go.
To the field
  of Shame.

She tells Mister Samir:
"All the women of Padaram
  come here.
All the girls of Padaram
  come here.

"Before sunrise
or after sunset
they come here
      to do...
  you know what."

Latika points her finger
toward the sky.
She says:
"It's the worst
when the moon
      is full.

"I hate the moon.
I wish
  I could bury it."

To Bury the Shame

Suddenly
Latika feels
very
tired.

It's
    exhausting
to say these
important things
that everyone
    stays silent
                about.

Her legs tremble.
Her lips tremble too.
But she forces herself
    to finish.

"You said to me:
An engineer is someone who builds
                        something useful.
I wanted to work like an engineer
    to build
    something useful.
For my sister Ranjini.
For my ammamma.
For my aunty Nita.

"So that little kids,
other little Jamals,
   will never get infected
   with parasites
   that stop them
   from chasing chicks,
   that stop them
   from growing up.

"I wanted to work like an engineer
   to build
   something useful
   for myself.
Something
   to bury
   my Shame."

Latika takes
a deep breath:
"The pick…
The planks…
This hole…
All this
   was
      to build
         a
            toilet."

A Piece of Gum for Two

Mister Samir puts his hand
        in his pocket.
He takes out a stick of gum.
"It's my last one. Shall we share?"

Without waiting for an answer
   he breaks the stick in two.
One half for Latika.
One half for himself.

Mister Samir
asks Latika:
"Did you ever think
   that the moon
        could be
      your friend?"

Latika doesn't answer.
    A friendly moon?
She doesn't think so.

Mister Samir adds:
"The moon can be your ally
   can help you avoid holes
      or
see other dangers
such as...
        scorpions!"

The very-important-government-official
looks at the field
of Shame
and tells his secret:
"Ever since I was small
I've been
scared stiff
of scorpions.

"If I had to come
here
each night
and face the risk
of a scorpion's sting
I would also
borrow a pick
or two."

Mister Samir tells Latika:
    "You are a very
    brave
    girl."

Mister Samir smiles.
He smiles
    with his lips
            AND
    with his eyes!

When she sees
    this smile
Latika starts to
            laugh
            AND
            cry.

Life Goes On...

Padaram returns to its routine.
The big banyan tree blossoms.
The rice grows taller.
Chicks become chickens.
Life goes on.

Latika doesn't have to hurry
   anymore
in the morning.
She doesn't have
to take the long
way to the river
to avoid
the silly
carefree boys.
She simply fills
     her jug
    at the well.

Her ammamma has no fever anymore
but is still too weak
        to walk.

Her aunty Nita
has stopped crying
but she still repeats
the same sad sentences
the same useless wish.

Ranjini has stopped
kicking the hens
   on the road
kicking the goats
   on the road
kicking the dust
   on the road.

But…
Ranjini hasn't started
            laughing
              or
            singing.

The village women
continue
   to go
each night
to the field
   of Shame.

Each night
Latika continues
      to gripe
   and grumble.
She continues
         to wish
      she could
         bury
          the
         moon.

Return of the Gigantic Red Truck

Then
one beautiful morning
   the gigantic
   red truck
   returns to Padaram.

The village children
gallop to the truck
as excited as wild goats.

108

Latika jumps up.
The peas
    she was shelling
        roll in the dust.

She sprints
almost as fast
        as the wind.

A stranger
    in a white shirt
        gets off
the gigantic truck.

Oh no!
No!
No!
Latika doesn't hide
    her dissatisfaction
            and
    her disappointment.

This man does not wear
        a tiny polka-dot
                bow tie.
This man does not smile
    with his lips
    or with his eyes.
This man is not
    Mister Samir.

Latika pinches her arms
        so she won't cry.

The village sarpanch
tells the stranger from the city:
"Welcome to Padaram."

Strict and unsmiling
the stranger asks:
"Where is the girl called Latika?"

The sarpanch
    shakes his head
    from side to side.
He hesitates between
    astonishment
            and
    resentment.

Latika freezes.
She doesn't dare speak.

Quietly
Latika moves closer to Ranjini.
Quietly
the big sister
takes her little sister's hand.

The official from the government
gives Latika a letter
    and says:
"Mister Samir wanted
    to come himself
        but he had to go
    to the capital
    for his work."

Latika opens
    the letter
    with trembling
    hands.
The words
    on the paper
        jump
            before
                her tearful
                    eyes.

Ranjini gently
takes the letter
from her sister.
She reads it aloud…

With Great Admiration

Dear Latika,
I congratulate you
   for wanting to be an engineer.

I congratulate you
   for your ambition to build something useful.

You were very brave
to talk about these
important things
that everyone
   stays silent about.

You dared to name
         the Shame.
I congratulate you
   for your courage.

Dear Latika,
The moon is too beautiful to bury.

I'm sending you wood and bricks to build…
you know what.
I hope that will help you
   learn to love
      the moon.

With all my admiration,
Mister Samir

Chase Away the Shame

From the gigantic red truck
the village men unload
      concrete blocks
      bricks
      wooden planks.

The sarpanch asks:
"What is all this for?"

For the first time
the official from the government smiles.
He says:
"Latika can tell you better than I can."

This time
Latika refuses to be silenced
      by the sarpanch's furious frown
         and
      fists on hips.

She announces
  in a clear and strong voice:
"All this
will be used
to build toilets!
All this
will be used
to chase away
  the Shame!"

Friendly Moon

High
in the shimmering sky
   the silver
      moon
      gazes
         at a
      gleeful
      girl.

Head back
smiling
with her lips
   and
with her eyes
   Latika
      blows
         kisses
            to the
               moon.

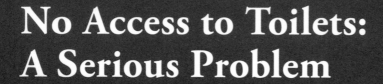

No Access to Toilets: A Serious Problem

In North America, almost everyone has access to toilets. So it's hard to imagine that many people in other parts of the world have to relieve themselves outside, in the fields, in a bush or at the end of an alley. Yet it's a very common situation.

More than half of the world's population has no access to toilets. This means that 4.2 billion people on the planet have no bathroom at home, or only have latrines or outhouses without running water, which prevents them from safely disposing of feces.

It also means that more than 600 million people have to defecate outdoors. Many countries are struggling with this problem, including China, Ethiopia, India, Indonesia, Mozambique, Nepal, Niger, Nigeria, Pakistan, Sudan and Yemen.

Is there a connection between toilets and health? Absolutely. Toilets save lives by preventing the spread of deadly diseases linked to poor hygiene. When millions of people defecate in fields or streams, the environment becomes an open sewer. Feces contaminate water and cause diseases such as diarrhea, cholera, dysentery, hepatitis and typhoid fever. Every year, hundreds of thousands of children die from diseases due to poor hygiene or lack of clean drinking water.

Is there a connection between toilets and safety? Absolutely. Without toilets, girls and women have to wait until nightfall to defecate and often travel a long way to the fields where they relieve themselves. This exposes them to various dangers such as venomous snakes, scorpions or being assaulted.

Is there a connection between toilets and education? Absolutely. One in five schools in the world doesn't have toilets. This becomes especially problematic for teenage girls, who are often forced to leave school when they start menstruating.

Stopping school at such a young age has serious consequences, because the more educated a woman is, the better equipped she is to take care of her children and earn a living. The connection may seem strange, but access to toilets and clean water is one of the solutions for reducing poverty.

For many people, toilet is a taboo word. However, if we talked more about the lack of access to sanitation, we could begin to address this injustice that affects billions of people.

World Toilet Day takes place every year on November 19. This event aims to raise awareness about an important public health issue.

Source: World Health Organization and UNICEF — 2020

Further Reading

World Toilet Day
worldtoiletday.info

"7 fast facts about toilets," UNICEF
unicef.org/stories/7-fast-facts-about-toilets

"The Crisis in the Classroom: The State of the World's Toilets 2018," WaterAid
washmatters.wateraid.org/publications/the-crisis-in-the-classroom-the-state-of-the-worlds-toilets-2018

"Living in a fragile world: the impact of climate change on the sanitation crisis," WaterAid
washmatters.wateraid.org/publications/fragile-world-impact-climate-change-sanitation-crisis

The Economics of Sanitation Initiative
wsp.org/content/economic-impacts-sanitation#top